Leabha

This book
belongs to:

_____

_____

_____

For Helen O'Neill
who is just like a third daughter

The Uninvited Guest

Frank Egan

Illustrated by Jeanette Dunne

WOLFHOUND PRESS

Published by
Wolfhound Press,
68 Mountjoy Square, Dublin 1.

This book is published with the financial assistance of The Arts
Council (An Chomhairle Ealaíon), Ireland.

British Library Cataloguing in Publication Data
    Egan, Frank
      The uninvited guest.
      I. Title
      823'.914[J]   PZ7

      ISBN 0-86327-082-4

Typesetting by Redsetter Ltd.
Printed by O'Brien Promotions Ltd.

CONTENTS

THE UNINVITED GUEST

Away back in time the Isle of Coosanure was the seat of the Árd-Rí (High King) of all the fairy kingdoms of Ireland. It was a beautiful island and to receive an invitation to attend one of its feasts or carnivals was a great honour indeed. Alas! because of a spell, the island sank to the bottom of the lake and is there to this day, silent and empty. However, thanks to our storytellers, we know something of its past glories and of the wonderful carnivals held there long ago.

One of the most popular stories was "The Uninvited Guest" and if we sit back, and are very quiet, we can hear Finn of the Roads, as he tells it.

Once upon a time, long, long ago the Árd-Rí sent out his Messengers to every kingdom in the land with special invitations to attend a great carnival. It was to honour his son Dara who was to wed on the great feast of Bealtaine on the lovely Isle of Coosanure. Nothing was spared – no work too hard to make the event one of great happiness for all who attended and to all who would hear of it in song and in story down the years.

The Árd-Rí had two children, Prince Dara and Princess Orla. Orla the Fair, as she was called, was a girl of great beauty and needless to say, she had many offers of marriage. Her father wished her to marry but she kept refusing all the offers for her hand. She liked Prince Cormac of Carrick Mór but she did all she could do to avoid him because she did not wish to hurt his feelings by saying "No" to his proposal; you see, Orla was deeply in love with someone else. Nearly a year ago, she was present at the great festival of Bealtaine at Clonfin. It was there she met a tall, handsome, young prince with whom she fell in love. He was very quiet and shy and while other young princes danced and made merry he was often content to sit with her and watch. When the others teased him about Orla he just smiled and said nothing. At first she felt sorry for him but soon began to realise that she was in love with him. Day after day during the Carnival she sought his company, so much so that the young princes began to tease her, too. She pretended not to notice, but secretly enjoyed their banter.

9

One morning, to her dismay, she found out that he had left the castle very early and gone back to his home far away. At first she was very upset because he had not come to see her to say good-bye. She knew in her heart, although he never said so, that he loved her as much as she loved him. She would tell no one. That would be their secret until they met again. A year had passed and although they did not meet again she still held on to her secret dream.

Her father suspected that she had a reason for not accepting one of her many suitors, but had no idea as to what the reason was. Little did he think as he drew up the list of invitations that he was going to bring the Prince and Orla together in a most remarkable way.

THE INVITATION

One of the Árd-Rí's messengers set out on the long journey to the North. He carried a special invitation to Niall, Prince of the Rosses in the lovely hills of Donegal. The Rosses was a very poor kingdom – so poor that the prince seldom went visiting as other young princes did. He was content to stay at home and live quietly, sharing the everyday life of his subjects. It came as a great surprise when the Árd-Rí's messenger arrived. Prince Niall received him with great respect, ordered the best rooms to be prepared and entertained him as befitted his high office. He felt honoured that the Árd-Rí had invited him and he assured the messenger that he would attend the feast. He would honour the Árd-Rí and the bridal pair but did not say what his gifts were to be. The messenger could not but wonder where the gifts were to come from. Gifts to the Árd-Rí must be of pure gold, be they great or small, and there were no signs of wealth here. Despite their gracious ways and great hospitality he could see that they were very poor indeed.

Still – they made his stay a memorable one. His rooms were comfortable and clean, his meals, although simple, were beautifully cooked and served with great taste. In the evenings he was entertained with songs – slow, sweet songs. He danced to their wild music and afterwards, their storytellers told of one-time deeds of glory in their lovely hilly kingdom.

When the time came for the messenger to leave he felt very sorry for them because they were so poor. He had come from a palace that was lavish and rich, yet he felt a great happiness with these people and their simple way of life. He had been treated with great respect and he promised himself that on his return to Coosanure he would ask the Árd-Rí to do something to help

them. He knew, too, that he would have to be most careful as they were a very proud people.

When the messenger had gone Prince Niall shut himself away in his room. As he sat there all alone the memories of another feast came back to him. It was nearly a year ago since he had been at the great carnival at Clonfin, where he had met and fallen in love with the beautiful Princess Orla. Instead of declaring his love he had left the palace secretly and returned home. From that day he had no real peace of mind. How could he, a poor prince, even think of love and marriage with the most beautiful girl in fairyland, and the daughter of the Árd-Rí? It was a foolish dream, but a dream that he could not forget – she was never far from his thoughts. He had promised himself that he would never again leave his kingdom, but now, out of the blue, had come the invitation. He accepted, of course. It was a great honour to him and to his people, but deep in his heart he knew that the real reason for acceptance was that he wanted to see Orla again.

THE GIFTS

Soon after the messenger had left, Niall called all his subjects together. He told them of the great honour bestowed on him and on them. He had accepted the invitation and told them that he would have to bring fitting gifts to the Árd-Rí and to the bridal pair in whose honour the feast was being held. If they were agreeable he would like to present the Árd-Rí with the Golden Collar of the Rosses. The Collar had lain in the treasury for hundreds of years. It was beautifully designed, of pure gold, and a fitting gift for a king. Even in their poverty it had remained part of their small treasure and nothing would tempt them to sell it to ease their poor state. But this was different. Their prince and themselves were greatly honoured and all agreed that their gift should be the Golden Collar of the Rosses.

When Niall mentioned gifts for the bridal pair there was silence. There was very little gold in the treasury and Royal gifts had to be of gold. The matter was discussed and debated for days and days but no one had come up with an answer to their problem. Then one day an old woman asked to see Prince Niall and being admitted to his presence, said, "Prince, I am old – very old, and expect the "Blink" at any time. (Fairies do not die – there is just a "blink" and they are gone forever.) I have no use for this gold brooch. Take it and have it melted down to make a link for a pair of golden chains for the bridal pair. If others would do the same then you could have chains that would bind their love for ever." Niall was deeply moved by this generous offer which, when it became known, was followed by so many

other gifts, that very soon there was enough gold to make the bridal chains. Now their Prince Niall could go to Coosanure and uphold the good name of the Rosses.

Soon it was time for Niall to set out on his long journey to the Isle of Coosanure on Lough Rí. He could not bring servants with him as they had no clothes fit to appear before the Árd-Rí. He would set out on foot – his only companion a small pony to carry the case containing his own court clothes and the Royal gifts.

THE JOURNEY

Leaving himself plenty of time to arrive on one of the "gathering days" Prince Niall moved slowly south, sleeping in the open – eating by the roadside. The weather was kindly at first, then it turned to rain. One day it rained very heavily, so heavily that he was forced to seek shelter for the night. Coming to a crossroads he saw a big house not too far away and decided that he would ask for food and a bed for the night. He approached the house and had to knock several times before the big door opened. Standing there before him was a man so much like Niall that anyone could take them for twins – same size – same build – same looks. Yes, they looked just like identical twins.

"I seek food and shelter," said Niall. "Can you pay?" said the man. "You look too poor to pay for anything!" Niall took out his purse, opened it and took out a gold coin. "Here is money," he said. "I need food and shelter for the night." He spoke very gently and the man, who suspected that this was no ordinary traveller, said "Who are you and where are you going to?" Somehow Niall did not trust him, so he said, "I am a weary traveller seeking food and shelter and I am willing to pay for your trouble." The man took the gold coin and showed Niall to a room. He saw other gold coins in Niall's purse, coins he would like very much to have. He left Niall, intending to return when his guest was asleep.

The room was not very clean with a small broken-down bed in one corner. Niall went outside to stable and feed his pony, returning with the case containing his clothes and the Royal gifts. All this did not go unnoticed by the man who watched Niall's every move. Rather than sleep on the broken bed Niall decided to sleep in his sleeping bag on the floor. The man – whose name we do not know, so we shall call him "Meaney" – brought in some hot soup and bread. Very soon Niall was fast asleep. He awoke very early in the morning feeling cold and weak. He got up and made his way to

the door intending to ask for something hot to eat and drink. When he opened the door he saw Meaney standing outside. Before Niall could say anything Meaney said, "I was just preparing a meal. If you want hot milk and porridge you had better come and get it". Niall was delighted as he made his way to the kitchen. After the meal he went back to the room and lying down, was soon asleep.

He did not waken until late in the day and when he tried to rise he could only do so after a great effort. Calling out to Meaney, he said, "I feel very tired and weak. I had better stay another night!" "You can stay as long as you like," said Meaney, "as long as you can pay! Go back to sleep and later I'll bring you a hot drink which will help you." After a while Niall slept and while he was sleeping Meaney entered the room, opened the case and saw the invitation, the Court clothes and the Royal gifts. With a sly smile he left the room.

Later he came back again and wakened Niall. "Here," he said, "drink this and the fever will leave you. I'll be back with a hot meal later on – but first you must drink this – all of it." When he left Niall drank a little of the liquid. It was sweet and pleasant to drink but Niall did not trust this man so he poured most of the drink down a crack in the floor.

No sooner had he done so when Meaney came back. Seeing the empty cup on the floor he started to laugh – a low mean laugh. Niall felt very drowsy and could barely hear the man say, "Oh, my Prince of the Rosses – for that's who you are. You will sleep now and for a long time. I will take your place at the feast. We look so much alike that no one will ever know. I'll have a great time at the feast and when it's over I will invite myself to this kingdom and that kingdom – to this palace and that palace. After all, the Prince of the Rosses will have to be treated with great hospitality so I will not have to worry about where I sleep or what I have to eat. I will not be coming back to this old place. When you wake up you will believe that you are me and never go back to the Rosses. You can have this house," and he laughed his low mean laugh.

All during this time Niall could only stare at Meaney. He knew now that the drink was magic and was glad he had only taken a little, but even that little took effect and he fell into a deep sleep.

Meaney left the room, taking all Niall's belongings with him and leaving his own ragged clothes behind on the floor. He washed carefully, dressed in his best clothes and made ready for the long journey. He took the case with the court clothes and gifts and as he was not coming back to this old place he took with him his hoard of gold. He packed all on the pony's back and set out for the Isle of Coosanure.

THE ARRIVAL

Two days later, on the first of the "gathering days", Meaney, now pretending to be Niall, Prince of the Rosses, arrived at the shore of the great lake. He could see the beautiful island with its great castle in the distance and was wondering how he was going to get across. Crafty man that he was, he soon solved the problem to suit himself. He had no further use for the pony so he traded it with a man who took him over in a boat. When he arrived at the castle gates he showed the invitation and was admitted. A servant came along and took him to a room where he would sleep during his stay on the island. Meaney was very tired and after a little snack, lay down and was soon asleep.

He was wakened early in the evening and told that in an hour's time he would be presented to the Árd-Rí, and then afterwards taken to the first of the great feasts.

Meaney dressed carefully in the court clothes and putting on the Golden Collar he left the room. You see, he had decided to keep the Collar for himself. He knew he had to give a gift to the Árd-Rí so he said he'd give him the bag of gold coins that he had taken from the prince at the house on the crossroads. As for the bridal chains – well, he might like to keep them too. He would decide later on. As he walked away from his room a servant waited on him. "Come, Prince of the Rosses, I will take you to the throne room, and the messenger will present you." Down along many corridors they went and arrived at the doors of the big throne room. As it was the first of the "gathering days" there was quite a crowd waiting to be presented to the royal family. Meaney looked around and was pleased to see them all admiring his Golden Collar and was glad that he had decided to keep it for himself. As he moved in line towards the throne, a messenger came forward

with hands outstretched in welcome. "I am so glad to see you again", he said. "I have told the Árd-Rí about you and your people. He is looking forward to seeing you. We hope to repay you for the pleasant visit to your kingdom!"

Meaney was very pleased with himself as he thought, "If this messenger does not know who I really am, it will be easy to fool the others". He thanked the messenger for his kind welcome and soon it came to his turn to be presented to the Árd-Rí and his family.

Let us go back a little in our story. You remember that Niall was Orla's secret love. She was seated beside the queen and could see the tall, handsome figure come nearer and nearer. She could hardly sit still and was so proud when she heard the court official announce, "May I present Niall, Prince of the Rosses!"

When the Árd-Rí heard the name he stood up and came down the steps. "Welcome, Prince of the Rosses. Welcome to our palace and our court. We have heard of your great hospitality to our messenger. We hope to repay your kingdom." He then presented Meaney to the royal family, whilst the big crowd clapped and cheered. Meaney bowed to the queen, winked at Dara and all but ignored Orla. What a shock she got! How could he treat her in such a manner? As she sat there, her mind in a whirl, she hoped that no one would notice how upset she was. She could hear Prince Niall make a fine speech, thanking the Árd-Rí for the great welcome he had received. Then she was horrified to see him produce a small bag of coins, and with a great flourish present it to the Árd-Rí. She heard the gasp from the crowd and then the awful silence in the room. The Árd-Rí stared at the man he believed was Prince of the Rosses as if he could not believe what had happened. A prince presenting his Árd-Rí with money! The man must be mad!

The Árd-Rí turned his back on Meaney, beckoned to the queen and with Dara and Orla they left the now silent room. As they walked down the long passage Orla could hear her father call out for the court officers. She knew he was very upset by what had happened. She was upset too but for a very different reason. She excused herself and fled to her room. She closed and locked the door behind her and walked to the window overlooking the lake. Was she a foolish girl with a foolish dream? No, she could not be that foolish. She felt that there was something wrong even as she said, "Niall, oh, Niall, why did you change so much? It's not like you, it's not like you."

Meanwhile back in the throne room whispering and murmuring went on. After such a great display of loyalty and friendship – how could the prince make such a blunder, be the cause of such an insult to the Árd-Rí?

All in the room felt very ill at ease and soon those who had welcomed Meaney moved away and then he was all alone. He wondered what had happened. If he was a real prince he would have known – but he made light of it. He was a guest and he was hungry and was looking forward to the coming feast. Nothing else worried him and as the trumpets called out he followed the crowd towards the great dining hall. The smell of rich cooking made his hunger all the greater and entering the hall he took a seat near to one of the doors leading to the kitchen. He was making sure that he would be among the first to be served. Little did he know what was in store for him. Had he known, he would have left the hall and the island, gone back to his crossroads home and begged forgiveness from the prince he had so cruelly wronged. But, he did not know and just now his mind was on food – gorgeous rich food, and plenty of it.

THE FIRST FEAST

When the Árd-Rí and his messenger had spoken to Meaney both thought that he was Niall of the Rosses. However, when Meaney presented the money to the Árd-Rí both knew that there was something wrong – very wrong. When the Árd-Rí left the room, he called his ministers to the state room and discussed all that had happened from the arrival of his messenger in the Rosses to the scene in the throne room. All agreed that something should be done, and done very quickly.

The Árd-Rí sent for his chief magician, told him what had happened in the throne room and asked him to use all his powers to find out the truth before the first feast began. The magician said "If the man is not the real prince, the Árd-Rí will be told, and I will make this man very sorry he has ever come to the palace. Then, I will have the real prince at the wedding feast on the third night." True to his word, he did find out that Meaney was not the real prince. He told the Árd-Rí and then made secret plans for a real magic feast for Meaney.

The first of the feasts began – every seat was filled. The tables were laden with food and drinks of every kind. Musicians played soft, sweet music. Waiters moved quickly among the guests asking them their fancy for the first course. Meaney sat between two princes but did not address them. He shouted at a passing waiter. "Hurry up there. I'm starving!" The waiter told him, "I will look after you. I am your *special* waiter." Meaney did not notice the gleam in his eye. Very soon the waiter returned with a big basket of delicious fruit. Meaney grabbed, first a pear and then a peach. He took a big bite of the pear, started to chew it and then suddenly spat it out – it tasted just like scented soap. He bit into the peach and spat it out too – it tasted like a lemon. He tried the other fruits, strawberries like salt, grapes like sloes, apples like vinegar. "Terrible! Terrible!"

He was about to protest to the waiter coming towards him, but when he saw the waiter was bringing him soup – lovely soup, that he could smell even from a distance – he said nothing. The waiter placed the big bowl of soup before him and some rolls beside the bowl. Meaney grabbed the rolls, tried to break them but could not. They were just as hard as stones. He threw them down on the table and after taking a spoonful of the soup which proved to be delicious, he dropped the spoon and did the most awful thing. He took up the bowl in his two hands and began to slurp the soup in great mouthfuls. Imagine his surprise when after swallowing a few mouthfuls of the lovely soup it had turned into a sour evil-smelling liquid. "I'm poisoned," he cried. "That was awful." He threw the bowl down on the table spilling the contents. He looked around and was surprised to see the other guests enjoying their soup. "What was wrong with mine?" he said to himself. At that moment the waiter appeared and without a word, took away the upturned bowl and the rolls.

Meaney was too shocked to say anything and when the waiter returned a little later to ask Meaney if he would like the fish course, a fresh salmon, he decided to say nothing just then. Meaney loved salmon, but seldom ate it. It was too dear to buy and he never got it from his friends. "Yes," he said, "I love salmon; if it's fresh bring plenty of it. I'm starving." "Yes," said the waiter, "it's fresh, very fresh!" The waiter then brought along a lovely salmon on a silver dish. Meaney grabbed a knife and fork. He was about to plunge the fork into the salmon when he heard a low growling voice. "You wouldn't dare, you low commoner!" Meaney looked around quickly at the two princes thinking that one or the other had spoken, but no, both of them were in conversation with the guests on either side. "Must be hearing things," said Meaney, plunging the fork into the side of the salmon, and was about to cut a big slice when he heard the voice again. Looking down at the silver dish he saw the salmon looking at him through big beady eyes, its mouth moving in an awful way. "Pull out that fork and leave down that knife," it said, "or I will tell everyone who you are. Only a real prince may eat Royal Salmon. It's bad enough been eaten by royalty, but to be eaten by you, you low commoner."

Meaney went pale. He tried to hush the salmon but the more he tried the louder it shouted. Pulling out the fork and throwing the knife down on the table, he called the waiter. "Take this away," he said, "I've lost my taste for fish. What's for the next course?" "Would you like roast duck?" said the waiter. "Oh yes, bring in two of them and all the trimmings." As the waiter took away the dish Meaney could hear the salmon starting up again. "Low commoner, you are no prince." Looking around in horror to see how the other guests were taking all this he was relieved to see that they were chatting and talking among themselves and had not heard that loud-mouthed salmon. He sat back and began to think, but he was so hungry that he could not think clearly. Here he was, fruit, soup and fish courses over, and he had not had a decent mouthful of food. He would speak sharply to the waiter, but when he arrived with a big silver platter, he said nothing. On the platter he could see two roast ducks, golden coloured ducks, green peas, carrots, roast potatoes, a meal fit for a king or for a prince.

He forgot to question the waiter, he forgot his misery. He forgot what had happened earlier on, and grabbed the knife and fork. Without delay he plunged the fork into the nearest duck and lifted the knife to cut. Before he knew what was happening, the duck gave a sudden jump and with the fork sticking out of its plump breast, rose into the air with a loud "Quack! Quack! You low commoner," it screeched. "How dare you attack a royal duck from the royal pond. How dare you." It proceeded to quack up and down the table. Meaney in panic, seeing his meal about to vanish dropped the knife and grabbed the other duck. "This one will not get away!" he said, but before he could sink his teeth into the golden brown flesh, he heard another awful quack. The second duck jumped from his hands and shouted at the top of its voice, "No one eats me but royalty, and you are not royalty." It joined the other duck and wing in wing they marched up and down the table shouting, "We are royal and we stay royal."

Meaney panicked again. He grabbed a big spoon, tried to scoop peas into his mouth, but try as he might the peas would not stay on the spoon. He tried the carrots but they slid off the spoon. In desperation, he grabbed a roast potato. It let a loud scream. "Put me down, you low commoner. How dare you try and eat me – me, a royal potato! Put me down at once." Meaney dropped the potato, and stared in horror as it jumped off the platter and, calling to the others, led a procession of potatoes, peas and carrots up and down the table shouting at the top of their voices, "We were too well reared to be eaten by a low commoner. Royal vegetables for royalty. Down with the low commoner!" The two ducks now joined in the uproar. It was too much for Meaney. Looking around the room he saw that no one seemed to notice what was going on. Kings and princes were eating away, talking and chatting. Was all this a dream? Was he sick? He did not know for certain, but he knew what he must do. He jumped to his feet, pushed the waiter out of his way and fled from the room.

When he got to his room he sat on his bed and tried to understand what had happened. The more he thought the more confused he got. He knew what had happened but could not understand why no one seemed to notice. He sat there for a long time and then went to bed. As he lay there he said to himself, "Everyone accepts me as the Prince of the Rosses. But everyone seems so cool. I wonder if they know. But they couldn't, could they?" Just then the servant came in. "Your Highness," he said, "Is there anything you require?" Meaney was going to ask for a snack, but was afraid of what might happen. "No," he said, "I do not want for anything." He was very hungry of course but when he heard the servant address him as "Your Highness" he believed that no one knew his secret. With that little grain of comfort he fell fast asleep. Soon afterwards the servant came in and placed a blanket over the sleeping figure. It was a magic blanket and Meaney would not waken until an hour after the blanket was removed.

THE SECOND FEAST

Night passed, and all next day. Late in the evening the servant came, removed the blanket and waited for an hour before he returned to tell Meaney, "Your Highness, the feast will begin in an hour." Meaney arose, washed, dressed and left the room. More guests had arrived, and the place was crowded. He spoke to some of the guests. They answered politely, admired his Golden Collar from afar, but left him to talk to himself. Quite suddenly a little old man wearing a crown came up to him and spoke, "Oh, Prince of the Rosses, the feast will not start for some time yet. You have not seen the treasures of the palace. Come, let me show them to you." Before Meaney could protest, the man, who introduced himself as King Gream, took him by the arm and led him down a passage away from the dining hall.

Room after room was explored. Meaney was interested at first. All the time King Gream was laughing and joking, and behaving as if he was really enjoying himself. Quite suddenly he became serious. "Come, let us go back or we will be late for the feast." Meaney was delighted, but was very annoyed indeed to find that when they got back the feast was over, and the crowds were dancing and singing in the great hall. He turned nasty and attacked King Gream. "It's all your fault," he said, "I'm hungry, very hungry, and the feast is over. You and your treasures – what are you going to do about it?" King Gream started to laugh. "Don't be annoyed," he said. "Come with me and I'll get you all the food you want. You can eat as much as you like and as long as you like. Come with me." They went down a long passage and entered a small room. King Gream clapped his hands and a waiter appeared. It was Meaney's waiter of the night before. Without a word of greeting, he set a table, left and returned with a big tray of food. Meaney's mouth watered at the sight of so much delicious food. Forgetting good manners, and without waiting for King Gream to join him, he just grabbed the nearest food on the tray. Fruit cakes, cuts of meat, trifles, jellies, apple tarts. All went down as quickly as he could swallow them. Soon the plates were empty but he was not satisfied.

"More," he cried to the waiter. "More and much more." Soon the waiter returned with more and more and more. Meaney ate all before him and still called for more. King Gream laughed and joked all through the long procession of trays of food, but did not eat anything himself. Still Meaney was not satisfied. He ate all through the night and soon the dawn light was breaking through the windows. it was only then that Meaney realized that he had been eating all through the night and, strangely, he was still hungry. He turned to ask King Gream the reason but he was no longer there. He called the waiter and getting no reply he got up and entered the room from whence the waiter brought the food. There was no waiter and the room was bare, no tables, no food, nothing, just a big bare room. At first Meaney was surprised and then frightened. No King Gream, no waiter, no food and he was still hungry.

He went out into the passage. Silence, not a sound. All was over, the feast, the dancing and the singing. Frightened, he raced down the passages until he came to his room. Sunlight was pouring through the windows, when tired and hungry, he got into bed and fell asleep. Soon afterwards the servant entered the room, placed the magic blanket over Meaney and did not return until an hour before Meaney was to awaken. When Meaney finally woke up he felt exhausted and hungry.

THE THIRD NIGHT

Lying there, Meaney went over the events of the last few days. The house at the crossroads, the prince, the journey, the first feast, the night before. He was very confused and vowed that he was going to the Árd-Rí to complain about the way he was treated. After the feast he would leave and seek hospitality with some of the other kings and princes. He did not like the ways of this great castle. Another thing, he was not going to part with the bridal chains. Indeed he was even sorry that he had parted with the bag of gold to the Árd-Rí.

He was tired and hungry and had no wish to leave his bed but he had made up his mind to attend the feast. He had to make friends with kings and other princes so as to invite himself to their kingdoms. The servant came in and said, "Your Highness, you have an hour before the wedding feast. You must be in your place before the bridal pair arrive." Meaney arose and washed himself. He turned to get his beautiful clothes. Imagine his surprise, his horror, to see not his beautiful clothes but his own dirty, ragged clothes, the clothes that he had left to the Prince of the Rosses at his crossroads home. The Golden Collar was gone, as were the bridal chains. All were gone, vanished, gone! gone!

He sat back on the bed and putting his head between his hands, he gave himself up to thinking. For a long time he sat there. Slowly, very slowly, all became clear to him. All his life he had led a life that seemed strange to him now. He realised that he had acted selfishly and had been mean and cruel. He had no real friends, but how could one like him expect to have friends. He thought of the man he had left behind him. He would still be sleeping and would sleep for a long, long time. Now his mind flooded with memories, none of them pleasant. Slowly remorse set in. He was sorry for himself, sorry too, for all the pain and misery that he had caused others all his life, but most of all for the prince, who only wanted food and shelter and had been robbed and cheated not only of his belongings, but of his very name itself. And for what? For love of gold! He dressed quickly in his own ragged clothes, and called the servant. At first the servant did not know him and was about to call the palace guards. Meaney said, "I know you do not recognise me in these clothes. I am not the Prince of the Rosses as I claimed to be. I wish to confess all to the Árd-Rí, but first I wish to see the King's messenger. I wish to undo a great wrong. Please help me, but hurry, please hurry."

The servant, frightened now, ran from the room and meeting the King's messenger said, "Please come quickly, there is something the matter with the Prince of the Rosses." The messenger smiled a knowing smile and went at once to the Árd-Rí. Later on he returned and asked Meaney to tell him his story. Meaney was a changed man. He confessed everything, not sparing himself. He begged help for the prince at the crossroads. He would replace the golden gifts. He would do his best to undo the wrongs of his past life. The messenger listened with great attention and, kind man that he was, was glad that Meaney had confessed all and better still, wished to make amends. "I will help you," he said. "The Árd-Rí knows all, and is very angry. Confess all to him, leave nothing out. Tell him you wish to make amends for your way of life in the past and your treatment of the Prince of the Rosses. Had you not spoken as you have done now, you would have been banished from Ireland. You would have been placed in a golden boat, because of your love of gold, and the boat pushed out from land. You would have had to live with your gold, without food or friends. You would travel around Ireland forever and never set foot on land again. Such was the anger of the Árd-Rí that that was to be your fate, but if you do as I say, he may show you mercy."

"Come with me," he said, he in rich clothes, Meaney in rags. In the distance they could hear the sound of trumpets. All the guests and court officials from the castle were making their way to the throne room. Soon the room was crowded with only a narrow passage from the doors to the Árd-Rí's throne. Excepting those in the Árd-Rí's secret no one knew why they were summoned to attend.

Princess Orla certainly did not know. She had kept to her room since meeting the one she took to be Prince Niall. She was very upset by the way he had greeted her and had intended remaining out of sight until the wedding. The Árd-Rí had commanded that all be present and she had to obey.

As she sat there, her mind far away, she watched as a tall, ragged figure entered the room and with head bent, walked slowly towards her father's

35

throne. She saw him kneel and nearly fainted when she heard the pleading voice.

"Your Majesty, I beg of you to hear me. I beg forgiveness for a selfish, mean and cruel life. I have cruelly wronged many during my life but none more than the Prince of the Rosses. I have taken his gold and the golden gifts intended for you. Worse than that, I have stolen even his good name. I am sorry for the life I have led and will, if given the chance, make amends. I have enough gold to replace the Golden Collar and the bridal gifts, but I will have to spend all my life repaying so many for the way I have treated them. I came to your castle as an imposter and even begrudged you the gold coins I gave you instead of the Golden Collar which you should have received. I disgraced myself in the dining hall and again last night in the room where I had the night long meal. I know now how bad I have been. Here I can only say I'm sorry. Give me a chance to prove that. I will repay all." By the time Meaney had finished, most of those in the hall felt sorry for him.

Orla sat there, shocked by this awful confession. Her thoughts raced to her loved one in the house at the crossroads. She could not cry out or show her feelings. She was a royal princess and must act like one. Later she would tell her parents of her love for Niall, but now she could only sit in silence as the drama continued.

Meaney knelt there ragged, lonely, and full of remorse. Most of those who had heard him had pity for him but there were quite a lot who disliked him, and said so. The Árd-Rí then spoke slowly and with great authority. "You have led a mean life. You have done a great wrong to the Prince of the Rosses. You say you are sorry and will undo the wrongs of your life. What can you do to repay all those whom you have cheated and robbed? What will you do to repay the prince for the way you treated him or the way you tried to deceive us since you came to the Isle of Coosanure? Before you answer I may tell you that I will leave your judgement to the kings and princes present. They will decide whether your offer is acceptable or not. They will decide! I would not trust myself to pass judgement."

Meaney looked around. He felt different. With a great desire to do good rather than evil, he spoke with great sorrow and shame. "Your Majesty, in the presence of all, I promise to make amends to the Prince for every wrong I have done to him. I will visit his kingdom and beg forgiveness from his people. I will bring them gifts. All that I can do, by using my hoarded gold. If allowed to do so, I will go back to my crossroads home. There I will build a big house. It will be an open house to friend, stranger and traveller. No matter how poor, or lonely, they will be welcome to food and shelter at no cost to them if they cannot afford to pay. No one will ever be turned away. Give me a chance to prove myself. Give me a year and a day to do as I promise. Then I will come back to you and accept your judgement as to whether or not I have kept my promise." The Árd-Rí spoke again. "You have heard his offer; will you now pronounce judgement!"

As he spoke, there was a sudden commotion at the door of the throne room. All turned to see a man enter. He came forward – a majestic figure dressed in rich clothes, and carrying a cushion in front of him. On the cushion lay a golden collar – The Golden Collar of the Rosses. Kneeling before the Árd-Rí, he said, "Your Majesty, I, Niall, Prince of the Rosses, pledge loyalty to you. I present you with this Golden Collar on behalf of myself and my people, as a pledge of loyalty and love. To your son, the prince, and his bride, I present these chains which will link their love for ever." The Árd-Rí was deeply moved. He arose from his throne and approached the kneeling figure. "Arise, Prince Niall of the Rosses. You are very welcome to our court. You have done us a great honour. We accept your gifts in the same spirit of loyalty and love. We know that you have suffered a great wrong. The wrongdoer has confessed all, has made certain promises, and now awaits the judgement of the assembly." The mood of the assembly changed when one of those who had a great dislike for Meaney shouted, "Let us have judgement, he should be punished severely." There was a cheer from others who agreed with him, and they too wanted Meaney punished.

Before a judgement was arrived at Prince Niall raised his hand. Addressing the Árd-Rí he said, "I am sure I know how everyone here feels, but in honour of the great feast I beg you to show mercy to this poor man, who, through his greed for gold has done many wrongs to so many, to you, to me, but most of all to himself. Greed for gold has made honest men turn away from love of man, from love of neighbour, even from love of his very own. It has changed him. It can change any one of us if we let it. I, who have suffered at the hands of this man because of his greed, say I forgive him everything. If he needs help I will gladly give it." Turning to the asembly, he said, "Any one of us can fall, we may want a helping hand to rise. Give your hand to this poor man for he surely wants it now."

The Árd-Rí nodded wisely as he heard this plea for mercy but, as he had already asked the assembly to pass judgement, he said, "Kings and princes, you have heard. It is now your duty to pass judgement."

At this stage Prince Dara, who had followed every move, every word since Meaney entered the room, rose to speak. "Friends, you have come to Coosanure to honour me and my bride on our wedding day. You have

brought many gifts for which we thank you. You would do us a further honour by showing your mercy to this poor man. I agree with Prince Niall. Free him to the Árd-Rí for a year and a day!" The assembly was deeply moved by this double plea, one from the prince so cruelly wronged, the other from the prince whose wedding they had come to celebrate. They made a decision very quickly and soon were shouting "We agree to that! Free him to the Árd-Rí!" The Árd-Rí smiled wisely as he said, "You have been most merciful. I give him a year and a day."

Meaney could hardly believe what he had heard. He had expected punishment, and now this. On his knees and with tears streaming down his face, he said, "Your Majesty, I will not forget." To Prince Niall he said, "You have shown great mercy – I will not forget. Above all, I have learned that love of gold for its own sake is a poor thing compared with the love of man. I have made promises. I will keep them all my life." Smilingly, the prince took Meaney, and raised him to his feet.

As Meaney was being escorted from the room, the Árd-Rí turned to Niall. Catching him by the arm he said, "Prince Niall, we have much to talk about concerning you and your kingdom! Tonight you will join us at the Royal table as our special guest, but now I wish you to meet my family." Niall bowed to the queen who smiled her welcome. Dara stretched out his hands in greeting. Orla, face to face with her loved one, could not speak but her smiling eyes told all. As their eyes met they knew that they were meant for one another.

Later that night they sat together side by side at the wedding feast. Earlier they had gone to the Árd-Rí and the queen and told them of their love for one another. The Árd-Rí gladly gave his consent to their marriage and the wedding was to take place on the great harvest festival later in the year.

Meaney spent the night in his room where he had his first real meal since he came to Coosanure. Just before midnight, the Árd-Rí came to visit him. "We have learned many lessons tonight. I hope that we all profit from them. I have a present for you. Here is a 'homing stick'. No matter where you are, on the last stroke of midnight, it will bring you to your new crossroads home." As he handed the 'homing stick' to Meaney the first bell of midnight rang out. They held hands together, the Árd-Rí in his rich clothes, Meaney in rags, but both of them smiling. As the last of the bells rang out, Meaney found himself on the steps of his crossroads home.

True to his promise, he did build a new house, and was always on hand to provide food and shelter for the poor and lonely.